A Day At The Dentist's

by Ellen Weiss • illustrated by Kristine Bollinger

Program created by Parachute Press, Inc. Published by Marvel Books, a New World Company, 387 Park Avenue South, New York, N.Y. 10016
Printed in the U.S.A.
ISBN 0-87135-105-6

It was a sunny Saturday morning, and the dentist's office was already full of kids.

"Rex Malone, it's your turn," Anita, the dentist's assistant, called.

Rex looked up from his magazine. It wasn't hard to spot him. He was the biggest and tallest and strongest and bravest of all the kids in the neighborhood.

ADVENTURE

“I really need to finish this article about fishing for sharks in South America,” Rex said. “Why don’t you let Nicole go before me?”

“Okay,” said Anita. “Nicole, you can go in and see Dr. Green now.”

“Can I go in wearing my roller skates?” asked Nicole.

“Sure,” said Anita.

Nicole skated out of the waiting room.

A little while later, she was back again.

"Hey, Suzie, look what I got from the prize box," she said.

Suzie looked up from her comic book. "Wow, a bracelet!" she said. "Maybe I'll get one of those, too."

After Nicole left, Anita asked, "Are you ready to go in yet, Rex?"

"Suzie can go in before me," said Rex. "I just started this article about exploring the North Pole."

Suzie went in, bouncing her ball.

About twenty minutes later, she came out bouncing *two* balls.

Flip was on the floor, playing with his trains.

"Look what I got, Flip," said Suzie excitedly. "I got a new ball, and it glows in the dark!"

“I could use a ball like that,” said Flip, “to put in my boxcar.”

When Anita came out again, Rex didn't even wait for her to start talking.

"Flip can go before me," he said. "I want fo finish this crossword puzzle."

When Flip came out wearing two engineer hats, there was nobody else but Rex in the waiting room.

"Rex," said Anita, "I'm afraid Dr. Green and I have to eat our lunches. Would you mind coming back after lunchtime?"

"Not at all," said Rex.

Rex went home and fixed himself a nice big sandwich for lunch. Then he took a short nap, and then he did some muscle-building exercises.

After a couple of hours, he went back to the dentist's office.

The waiting room was full of kids again.

When Anita came out, Rex was still not quite ready to go in. He had some homework to do.

Spike went in, and came out with a yucky rubber bug.

"Bleeagh!" he said, waving it in Kathy's face.

"Eek!" said Kathy, shaking her curls. "Get that disgusting thing away from me!"

Spike just giggled.

"How about it, Rex?" said Anita.

"I just remembered, I have to go home for a few minutes and walk my dog," said Rex. "Kathy can go."

"Certainly," said Kathy politely.

Rex went home and got his dog, Bucky. He walked the dog for a few blocks, and discovered that he was outside Dr. Green's office.

Rex looked in the window. The kids in the waiting room were reading magazines, playing games, and talking together.

He stood and watched for a while, and then Bucky tugged on the leash and they walked home.

REX
12

By the time he got back to the office, it was getting late. Timmy was just leaving, twirling the new decoding ring he had gotten from the prize box.

“Well, hi, Rex,” said Anita. “You’re the last patient for the day. Are you ready to go in?”

“Well, actually,” said Rex, “Maybe I’ll wait till next week. I think I might hear my mother calling me.”

“You know, Rex,” said Anita with a twinkle in her eye, “some people are a little scared of going to the dentist—people who are perfectly brave about other things in life. Are you just a little scared?”

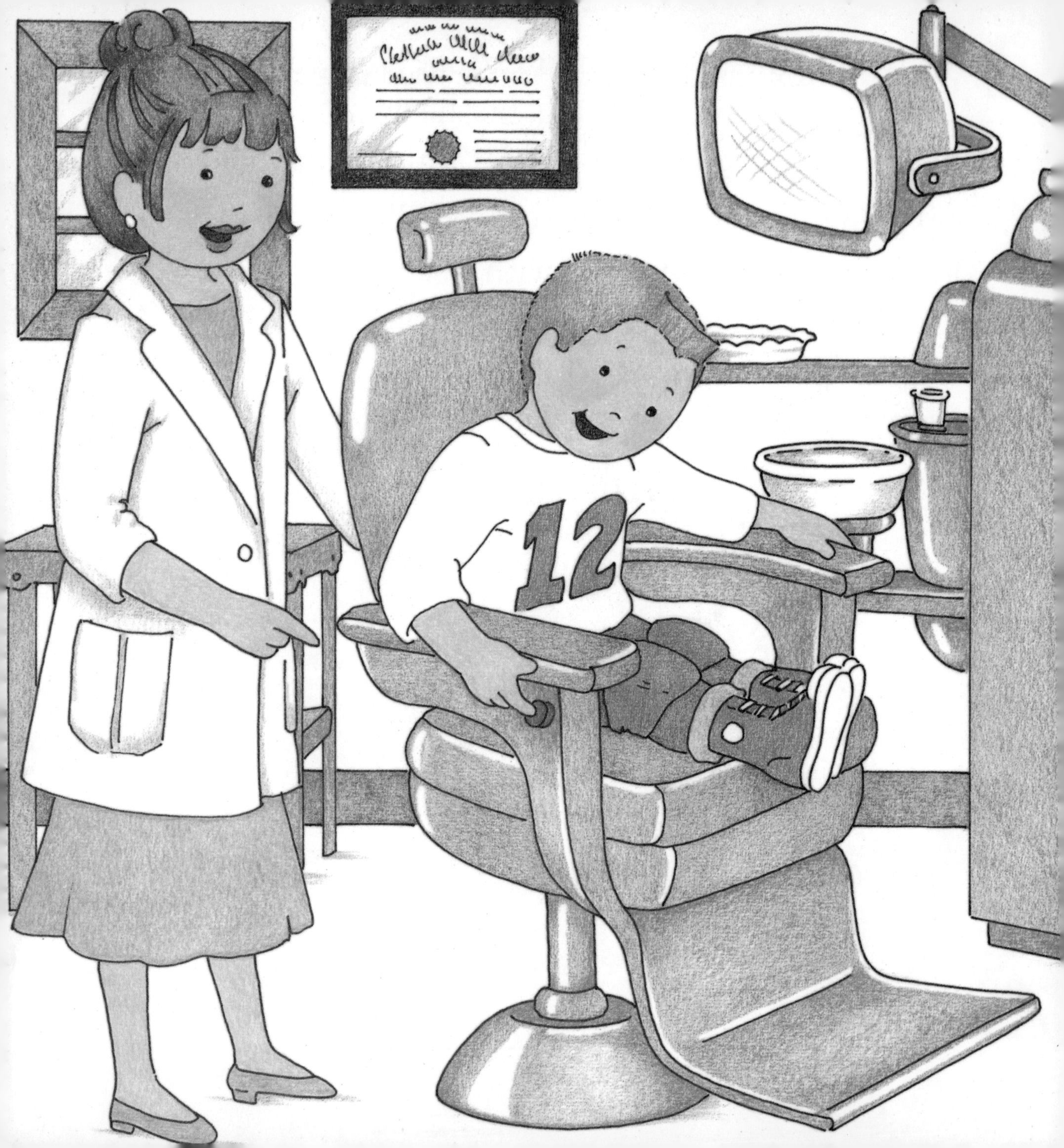
12

“Well—um—I guess so.” Rex took a big gulp. It was hard to admit he was scared, but he was.

“Know what I’m going to do?” said Anita. “I’m going to tell Dr. Green you need some extra-special attention. She won’t mind, since you’re the last one anyway.”

Dr. Green was smiling when Rex sat down in the dentist chair. “Would you like to raise it yourself?” she asked.

“Sure,” said Rex. He pushed the button until she told him to stop. It was a nice little ride.

Then she adjusted the light so it was shining in his eyes. “Sorry,” she said. “I need it to light up your mouth. Your eyes will get used to it in a second.”

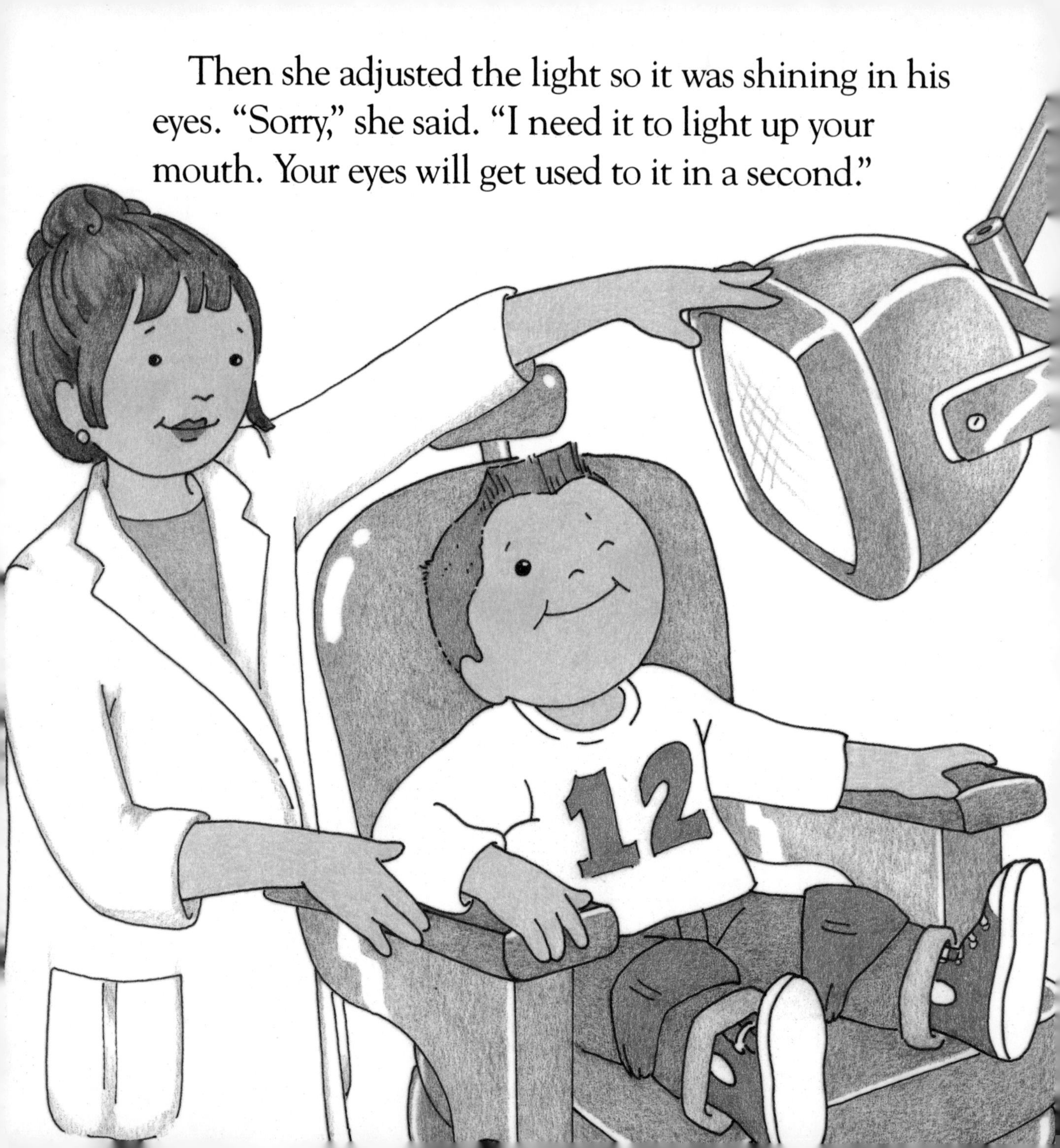

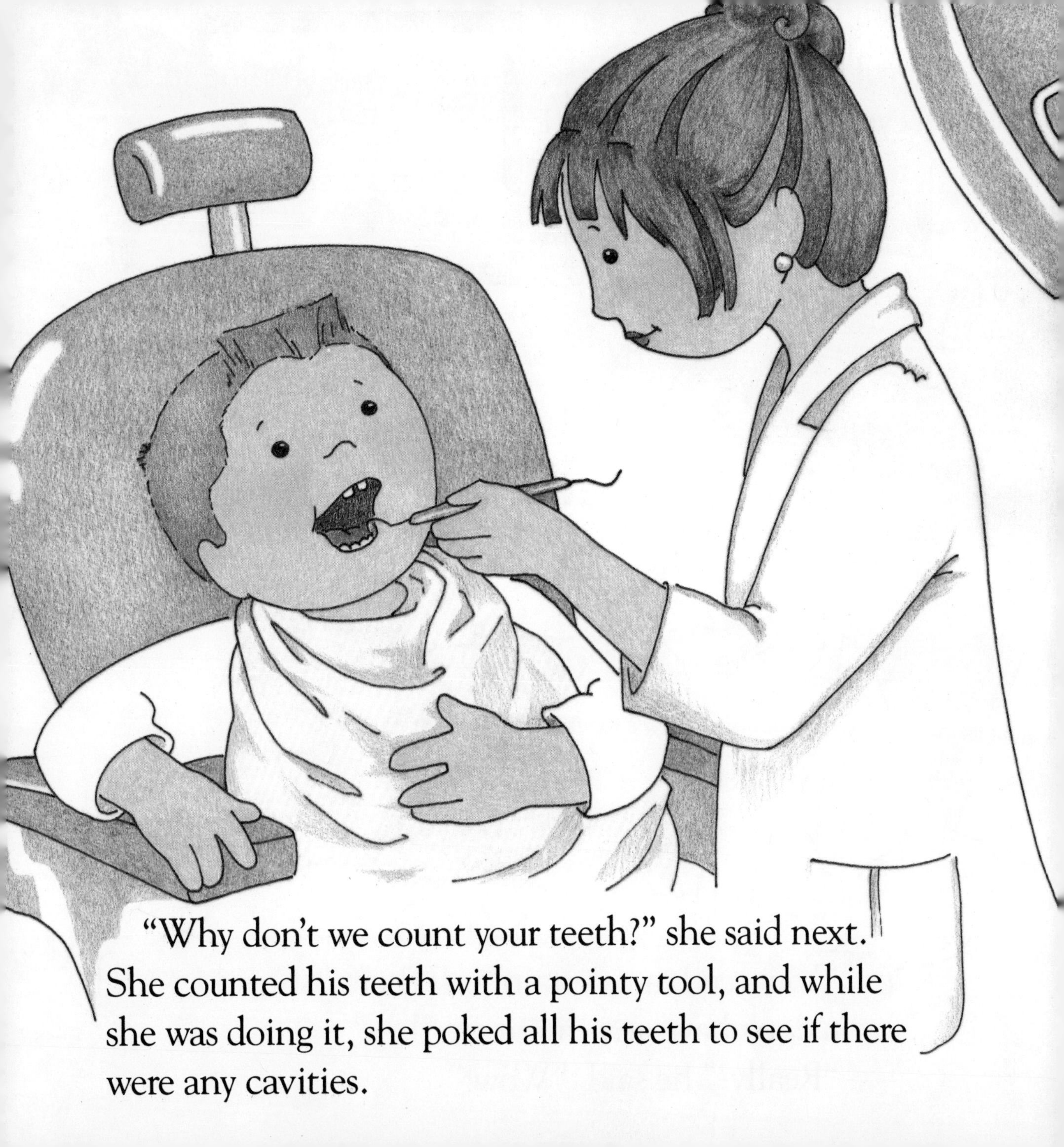

"Why don't we count your teeth?" she said next. She counted his teeth with a pointy tool, and while she was doing it, she poked all his teeth to see if there were any cavities.

"Your teeth are certainly all there," she said. "And you don't have any cavities, either."

"Really?" he said. "Wow!"

“Next I’m going to paint your teeth with fluoride, to help your teeth keep fighting cavities. Would you like strawberry, butterscotch, or peppermint?”

“Strawberry, please,” said Rex.

Rex settled way back in the dentist's chair, and Anita painted his teeth with strawberry-tasting stuff. "Don't swallow for a minute," she said. "You can hold the little vacuum cleaner that keeps your mouth dry, okay?"

Finally, Rex was allowed to rinse out his mouth. Anita gave him a big sticker with a smiling face on it. "Don't eat or drink for 30 minutes," it said.

"Okay, Rex, you're all done," said Dr. Green. "Would you like to pick out something from the prize box now?"

Rex felt a little old to be looking in the prize box, but he couldn't resist. And what should he find, right on top, but a nice little ball that he could throw for Bucky to fetch. "Thanks!" he said.

At last, it was time to leave. It was almost dark out.

As Rex stepped outside, he bumped into Clyde.

"Hi, Rex," said Clyde. "I see you were just at the dentist. My mom says I have to go, but I—I'm a little scared. How was it?"

"Nothing to it," grinned Rex, bouncing his new ball. "It's as easy as pie."